DESMOND COLE
GHOST PATROL

NIGHT OF THE ZOMBIE ZOOKEEPER

by Andres Miedoso
illustrated by Victor Rivas

LITTLE SIMON

New York London Toronto Sydney New Delhi

LITTLE SIMON

An imprint of Simon & Schuster Children's Publishing Division
1230 Avenue of the Americas, New York, New York 10020
First Little Simon paperback edition July 2018
Copyright © 2018 by Simon & Schuster, Inc.
Also available in a Little Simon hardcover edition.
All rights reserved, including the right of reproduction in whole or in part in any form.
LITTLE SIMON is a registered trademark of Simon & Schuster, Inc.,
and associated colophon is a trademark of Simon & Schuster, Inc.
For information about special discounts for bulk purchases, please contact
Simon & Schuster Special Sales at 1-866-506-1949 or business@simonandschuster.com.
The Simon & Schuster Speakers Bureau can bring authors to your live event. For more information
or to book an event contact the Simon & Schuster Speakers Bureau at 1-866-248-3049 or
visit our website at www.simonspeakers.com.
Designed by Steve Scott
Manufactured in the United States of America 0618 MTN
2 4 6 8 10 9 7 5 3 1
Library of Congress Cataloging-in-Publication Data
Names: Miedoso, Andres, author. | Rivas, Victor, illustrator.
Title: Night of the zombie zookeeper / by Andres Miedoso ; illustrated by Victor Rivas.
Description: First Little Simon paperback edition. | New York : Little Simon, 2018.
Series: Desmond Cole ghost patrol ; #4 | Summary: Desmond and Andres face a zombie
during a school field trip to the zoo. | Identifiers: LCCN 2017061716 | ISBN 9781534418042
(paperback) | ISBN 9781534418059 (hc) | ISBN 9781534418066 (eBook) | Subjects: | CYAC:
Zombies—Fiction. | Zoos—Fiction. | School field trips—Fiction. | Zoo keepers—Fiction. |
Friendship—Fiction. | African Americans—Fiction. | Hispanic Americans—Fiction. |
BISAC: JUVENILE FICTION / Action & Adventure / General. | JUVENILE FICTION /
Imagination & Play. | JUVENILE FICTION / Readers / Chapter Books.
Classification: LCC PZ7.1.M518 Nig 2018 | DDC [Fic]—dc23
LC record available at https://lccn.loc.gov/2017061716

CONTENTS

CHAPTER ONE

ZOOS ARE COOL

Everybody loves the zoo, right? Hey, who doesn't like cool animals? Who doesn't want to spend the day hanging out with lions, tigers, bears, and snakes? Okay, *maybe* not the snakes. They make my skin crawl.

But the rest of the zoo? Believe it or not, I'm just like every other kid. I love zoos!

I mean, where else can you see animals from all over the world in one place . . . *up close*?

Not to mention the merry-go-round, ice-cream stands, and a train that goes all the way around the park. Want to get from the apes to the petting farm without standing up? Then all aboard the Zoo Choo Train!

Zoos even have the coolest gift shops. They have huge stuffed animals and stretchy rubber snakes. Oh, in case you didn't know, I think fake snakes are fine. The gift shop also has T-shirts, magnets, and those

key chains with your name on it. Of course, they never have a key chain with "Andres" on it, so maybe I *don't* like the key chains so much. But still, the zoo is great.

I mean, it's kind of great.

Well . . . except for the snakes, like I said. Also, the zoo always has peacocks roaming free across the grounds. I have never trusted those peacocks. Why are they allowed to walk around? It's not like they are here to see the other animals.

I'll tell you what they are after: food. I had a bad run-in with a peacock one time. That sneaky bird stole a soft pretzel right out of my hand. And the pretzel was still warm!

And I'll never forget the time I spilled bird food all over myself in the bird habitat.

That did not turn out well.

Hmm, now that I think about it, once I was feeding a goat at the zoo . . . but the goat ate my video game instead of his real food.

Okay, maybe I shouldn't have been playing it *while* I was feeding the goat, but I was just about to beat my high score!

It's no wonder the animals are always looking for something new to eat. Have you seen what the zoo feeds them? Leaves, cold fish, and something called "pellets," whatever that is.

But none of that food is *half* as bad as what the zookeeper is carrying in that bucket now. It looks like something Desmond Cole's mom would make. Something she *has* made!

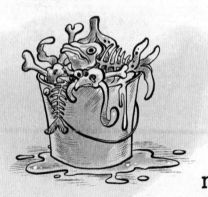

But that's not why Desmond and I are tailing this zookeeper. We're the Ghost Patrol. Maybe you can see us hiding right here. See, there is something odd about this zookeeper.

DESMOND COLE

ANDRES MIEDOSO

ZOOKEEPER'S LEG

CHAPTER TWO

THE LAST ROW

It was one of those days all kids look forward to.

Field trip day!

How cool was it that our class got to leave school while everybody else was still in their classrooms? And how *cooler* was it that we got to hop on a school bus while everybody else watched through the windows of Kersville Elementary?

I'll tell you: It was very cool! I mean, unless you're one of those kids who was stuck in class, of course.

Lucky for me, I wasn't one of them. And neither was Desmond Cole. We were going to the Kersville Zoo! This was my first field trip since I moved to town.

When you get on a school bus, everybody knows how important it is to choose the right seat. You have to pick the perfect one for the mood you're in. If you like bouncing, pick the row over the wheels.

If you worry about being carsick, sit in the front row because looking through the windshield will help the puke slide back down. And I should know. My parents say that I'm a pro at being carsick.

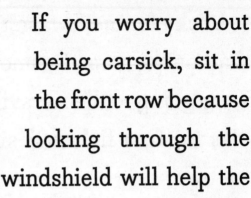

But that morning I felt great . . . and Desmond Cole was making a plan. Everybody knows that when you make a plan on a bus, there's only one place that will work: the last row.

"Okay, Andres," he said. "I worked on this plan last night. If we follow this map, we'll get to see as much of the zoo as possible. And we won't miss out on any of the best animals."

Desmond had spent a lot of time on this map. It had labels stuck all over it, and a trail highlighted in neon orange ink.

Desmond pointed. "Here's where we start, with the giraffes. Then we move on to the rhinos and elephants since they like to come out in the mornings."

"That makes sense," I said. I was impressed so far.

"Then we move on to the birds in the afternoon," Desmond said.

I nodded. "But we can't feed the birds," I reminded him.

"No problem," he replied. "We won't have time. Remember, we have to stick to the map."

18

PETTING ZOO

NIGHTTIME ANIMALS
17

GIRAFFES
1

ANTELOPE
15

BEARS
7

RHINOS
2

ELEPHANTS
3

BUFFALO
8

TIGERS
4

MERRY-GO-ROUND
14

LIONS
5

CAFETERIA
6

GIFT SHOP
16

INSECTS
12

SEALS
13

REPTILES
11

SNAKES SPIDERS

TICKETS

BIRDS
9

HIPPOS
10

19

That was when he told me the rest of his plan. As he talked, I got more and more excited. He had actually mapped out the perfect day at the zoo. We would even have time to go on the merry-go-round and buy stuff at the gift shop.

I was afraid Desmond might have a secret ghost plan hidden up his sleeve, but all he talked about was the zoo.

I leaned back and relaxed. It looked like we were going to have a normal, fun day at the zoo.

21

CHAPTER THREE

EAT NOW. EAT.

The best thing about the Kersville Zoo and my school is they believe kids should be able to explore and learn—*wait for it*—on their own!

I know! Crazy, right?

Of course, there were teachers and class parents on the trip with us.

And yes, we would still have to write a report about what we saw and learned at the zoo. But it was pretty cool that we didn't have to stick together the whole time. Instead, we had to stick with our buddy.

GIRAFFES

That was easy because my buddy was my best friend, Desmond.

While most of the kids headed for the bears, tigers, and lions, Desmond and I took off on our own adventure. We headed straight for the giraffes, just like we planned.

At the giraffe exhibit, there was a wooden platform surrounded by thick trees. It was hard to see anything other than the leaves. Then we spotted the giraffes. They were eating breakfast, if you could call a bunch of leaves "breakfast."

"Can you believe nobody else is around?" Desmond asked. "The last time I was here, it was packed! I couldn't even see over all the grown-ups. Some of them even had little kids on their shoulders. That was not fair."

We stood there and watched the giraffes. There were four adults and three young ones that were playing like a bunch of human kids.

Suddenly, I got an eerie feeling. It felt like somebody was on the platform with us. We weren't alone anymore!

That's when I heard a deep voice speaking slowly from behind me. "Eat now. Eat."

Desmond and I whipped around and nearly hopped onto the nearest giraffe's long neck! The voice belonged to a zookeeper, and he looked . . . different. Yeah, he was wearing the regular zookeeper uniform. He had the khaki shirt and shorts, and even a hat. But his eyes were big, and his skin was a weird greenish color.

Maybe he's not really green, I thought. *Maybe it's just a reflection from all these trees.*

Then the zookeeper said it again:
"Eat."

I swallowed hard and froze in place. *He wants to eat us!*

That's when I noticed he was holding branches of leaves.

"Cool!" Desmond said, taking one of the branches from the creepy zookeeper. "Thank you."

I didn't move a muscle.

"C'mon, Andres," Desmond said, nudging me. "We can feed these leaves to the giraffes!"

I breathed a sigh of relief. Sure, the zookeeper looked a little bit . . . green, but that didn't mean he was going to cat us. I took the other branch from him and tried to smile.

"Thanks," I managed to say.

The zookeeper stayed quiet. He just looked at us with an empty gaze.

Then Desmond and I waved the leaves as the giraffes came over to chomp the branches in our hands. I couldn't believe how close we were to them. It was amazing!

When all my leaves were gone, I noticed Desmond wasn't feeding the giraffes anymore. He was staring at the zookeeper, who was now walking away.

"Hey, Andres," he said. "How do you feel about changing our zoo

plan? I think we should go see the seals and penguins next."

That was where the zookeeper was headed. Desmond wanted to follow him!

Oh no, I thought. The Ghost Patrol had found another case.

SEAL EXHIBIT

CHAPTER FOUR

HOLD YOUR BREATH

Desmond and I pushed open the double doors to the seal area. The smell was like getting hit in the face with a bag of stinky cheese and rotten eggs . . . all soaked in vinegar.

"Oof!" I said, covering my mouth with my hand.

"What's that smell?" Desmond asked. His face was scrunched up.

"Seals," I answered. "They spend a lot of time in water, but they smell like they need a bath!"

The doors closed behind us, and we were swallowed up by the darkness. I held my breath. The only light was a murky blue-gray one from down a long corridor. Cold air blew on us as we walked toward the light.

Finally I asked Desmond, "What are we doing here?"

He whispered, "It's the zookeeper. There's something funny going on with him."

I shook my head. "Hmm, he looked a little scary, but he was nice. He gave us the giraffe food."

"I know," Desmond said. "But I still want to follow him, just in case."

I hadn't known Desmond all that long, but it was long enough to know that when his spooky alarms go off, he was always right.

When we got closer to the light, we saw that it came from a large window that looked out onto a murky blue world. The glass was covered in dirty smudges though, so it was kind of hard to make out what was inside.

But then there was a splash. It was water! Suddenly, we could see seals swimming and darting around! It was pretty awesome.

Desmond and I sat there alone. We couldn't take out eyes away from the seals.

SPLASH!

A seal swam around for a little while and then jumped back out onto the land above. Another seal followed and did the exact same thing. Maybe they were playing a game. It was fun to watch.

Desmond was still looking for the zookeeper, but he was nowhere in sight.

"Maybe we should go," Desmond said. He seemed disappointed.

Before I could answer, we heard—

SPLASH!

This time it wasn't a seal diving into the water. It was the zookeeper! He swam all the way to the bottom and stood in front of the window, looking right at us with the same blank expression he had before.

Then he pulled out a sponge and started cleaning the dirty window. After only a few wipes, the view was crystal clear!

"See, Desmond," I said. "He's just doing his job. There's nothing to worry about."

"Yeah, he's doing his job," Desmond said. "But he's doing it *underwater* . . . and he's doing it without any air!"

I gasped. Desmond was right. We both stood with our mouths hung

open in horror. I started to panic. The zookeeper was spending too much time underwater without any scuba gear or anything!

I could tell that Desmond and I were both wondering the same thing.

This isn't possible. How is the zookeeper breathing?

CHAPTER FIVE

SNAKES OR SPIDERS

It didn't take Desmond and me more than a few seconds to decide what we had to do. *Run!*

The problem was that I thought we were running *away* from the zookeeper. It turned out Desmond Cole was running *after* him.

Before I knew it, we were on the topside of the seal area. The seals were resting on rocks in the sun. Everything seemed really normal.

"Over there!" Desmond said, pointing to wet footprints on the ground that led toward the lion area. "Let's follow the zookeeper."

"But, um," I said, trying to change the subject. "What about your map? Maybe we should forget about the mystery and stick to your zoo plan."

Desmond grabbed my arm and pulled me. "We need to go now!"

The next thing I knew, Desmond

and I were running toward the lion exhibit. It looked like a forest with trees and huge rocks for the lions to rest on. We found a spot where we could spy on the zookeeper. He was *inside* the enclosure . . . right next to the lions!

First, we watched him feed raw
steaks to the lions. The crazy thing
was that he fed them with his bare
hands! I almost passed out whenever
a lion snapped at the meat. And each
time the zookeeper pulled his hand
back, he still had all his fingers!

Next, we followed the zookeeper to the hippopotamus area and watched him brush a hippo's teeth. Weird, I know. And then he flossed the hippo's teeth too. Gross!

Then we tracked him to the snake house and watched him go into the section with all the deadly snakes and collect their venom. It was terrifying! I would have fainted right there, but we were too close

to the spider exhibit. I did not want
to wake up wrapped in spiderwebs.
Now I couldn't decide which to be
more afraid of: spiders, snakes, or
this zany zookeeper. Ugh!

"I'm worried he's going to get hurt," Desmond whispered. "There's definitely something strange going on here."

Then I had a brilliant plan on how to make my escape. "We better go warn somebody," I said.

Desmond nodded. We ran out of the snake and spider areas and found another zookeeper. She was dressed exactly the same as the creepy zookeeper, but she wasn't green.

"Hey, kids," she said. "I'm Peggy. Are you enjoying the—"

"Wait! This is important," I cried, interrupting her. "We have to tell you something!"

And that's exactly what we did. We told her everything we had seen—

every single detail. Then we waited for her to tell us she was going to get to the bottom of this mystery. But that's not what happened.

All she did was reach into her pocket and pull out a pair of tickets. "You boys don't need to worry," she said, smiling at us. "Here are two free passes for the merry-go-round. Go have fun."

"But—" Desmond began.

"Run along," Peggy said, pointing us in the direction of the merry-go-round. "Just have fun. It's easy!"

Fun. Something told me having fun wasn't going to be as easy as it sounded.

CHAPTER SIX

THE DIZZIES

We found the merry-go-round. Nobody is too old for the merry-go-round at the zoo. Why? Because they have every kind of animal you could possibly want to ride. They don't just have horses. They have cute panda bears and wild tigers.

Desmond Cole, of course, wanted to ride the weirdest animal they had: a praying mantis.

Me? I rode the skunk because nobody messes with skunks, not

unless they want to walk away smelling worse than a bunch of seals!

Desmond and I were the only people on the merry-go-round. The man operating the ride gave us a nod, and then the ride started.

Desmond sat up on his praying mantis and looked out onto the park. "I wish this ride would go faster," he said. "We've got to find that zookeeper. I've got a hunch about him. Have you ever heard of zombies?"

I had to clutch the neck of my skunk just to keep from falling off.

"Z-z-zombies?" I asked. "Zombies that eat brains? They're real?"

"Maybe," Desmond said. "I think we may have found a zombie zookeeper."

"In that case, I think we should let him get away," I told Desmond.

But I knew Desmond wasn't the kind of kid who let mysteries like that go unsolved. Nothing stopped him. Not even zombies.

Desmond was on the case. There was nothing I could do.

So I tried to relax and enjoy this unzombied merry-go-round.

Everything was great at first. It was a nice, slow ride. Then we started picking up speed.

I gripped the pole tighter and held on for dear life as we spun faster and faster.

And faster!

When we zipped past the control booth, guess who was operating the merry-go-round?

The zombie zookeeper!

The ride picked up even more speed, and Desmond and I had to wrap our arms around our poles just to keep from flying off!

What is the zombie zookeeper up to?

We had only one chance to save ourselves! Still clutching our poles, Desmond and I jumped down from our animals and grabbed on to the animal next to ours. Then we grabbed the animal next to that one. Pretty soon we reached the safest, most *normal-boring* place on the merry-go-round: the sleigh.

The sleigh didn't go up or down. It just stayed put. Plus, even when the merry-go-round was spinning fast, being in the sleigh felt like you were barely moving. It's the place where all the parents and newborn babies sit.

Finally, the ride slowed down to a stop, but we had a bad case of the dizzies. It seemed like the zoo was spinning around us at top speed.

When I was able to focus again, I looked over at the controls box, and the zombie zookeeper was gone!

"We have to find him!" Desmond said.

"Um, 'we'?" I asked.

Desmond pulled me off the sleigh. "Come on," he said.

Desmond and I jumped off the merry-go-round . . . right smack into Peggy, the nonzombie zookeeper.

"Your class is having lunch now," she said. "Follow me to the cafeteria."

Desmond folded his arms. "But we were getting ready to—"

"Come along," Peggy said, ignoring him.

Desmond and I followed Peggy to the cafeteria.

Desmond might have been upset that he lost the trail of the zombie zookeeper, but I was happy. After what that creepy zookeeper had just put us through, I needed time to let my stomach settle back down.

CHAPTER SEVEN

PEACOCK PATROL

In the outdoor cafeteria, the entire class sat at picnic tables in the sunshine. We were even given hamburgers, french fries, and apples for lunch. I picked up my apple and began munching.

Desmond was eating so fast that

it looked like he thought someone was going to steal his lunch. That was when I remembered his mom's cooking and how he had to eat that food every night. Her food even gave *ghosts* tummy troubles. No wonder Desmond was eating this lunch so fast . . . and with a smile on his face!

All the kids were talking about the animals they had seen, but Desmond was still focused on only one thing. He pulled out his map and whispered to me, "We need to catch that zombie off guard. Someplace where he can't see us coming."

My leg started to shake under the picnic table.

Desmond pointed to an exhibit called Nighttime Animals. "Here!" he said. "This is a special show about nocturnal animals. Those are animals that only hunt at night."

I already knew this, but I had just

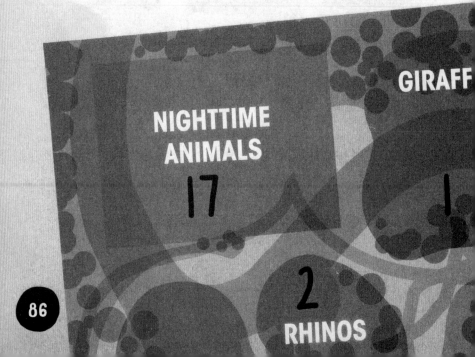

NIGHTTIME ANIMALS
17

GIRAFF

2
RHINOS

shoved a couple of french fries in my mouth, so I couldn't say anything.

Desmond continued, "I'm sure the zombie zookeeper will end up at this exhibit. And that's when we'll make our move."

"*Our*" move?

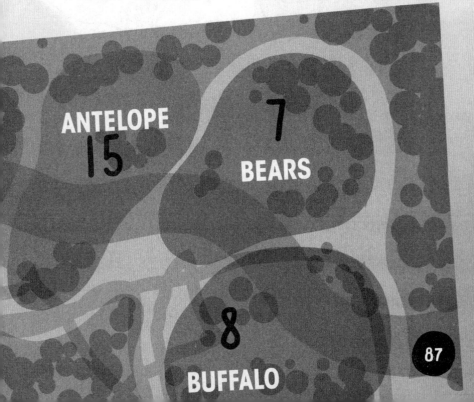

ANTELOPE
15

7
BEARS

8
BUFFALO

Desmond looked so proud of his plan, but I needed answers. "And what exactly is our move?" I asked.

But before Desmond could answer, a large rainbow of wings flapped open onto our table.

Oh no! A peacock! And it grabbed my hamburger!

"Not again!" I screamed as it flew off the table with my lunch.

Okay, I have to admit, chasing after a hamburger-snatching bird probably wasn't the best idea I'd ever had, but in my defense, I was really hungry.

As that bird took off with my meal, I jumped up and ran after it. No way

was I going to let a bird steal my food a second time!

But peacocks can fly! I don't mean "fly" like they move fast. I mean "fly" like with wings! That bird flew over a wall, and I was so determined to catch it, I scrambled over the wall right after it.

It wasn't until I landed on the other side that it occurred to me why zoos have walls. I was in the buffalo habitat.

Buffalo!

Suddenly, I was surrounded by a group of curious beasts. And that peacock sat right beside them, eating my hamburger and making a high-pitched noise.

It was *laughing* at me!

As the beasts came closer, I backed up against the wall.

That's when I felt a hand reach over the wall and pull me back to safety.

I turned around to say thanks to whoever saved me and came face-to-face with . . . the zombie zookeeper!

I heard a wail—
something that
sounded more
like a siren
than a scream.
And yes, that
sound had
come from me!

The zombie zookeeper might have saved my life, but I wasn't about to stick around to thank him. I ran back to my picnic table as fast as I could, still lunch-less.

No hamburger was worth that much trouble!

CHAPTER EIGHT

BUCKET OF SLIME

As we got closer to the exhibit, I could feel myself start to tremble.

NIGHTTIME ANIMALS:

NOCTURNAL ANIMALS OF THE WORLD

Even the sign was scary!

I have to tell you, being in the dark with animals *and* a zombie was not my idea of a good time. But the Ghost Patrol did what it had to do to get to the bottom of every mystery.

We stepped inside, and it instantly changed from day to night.

It was dark, but not *that* dark. I breathed a sigh of relief. Secretly, I hoped this plan wouldn't work, and we could finish our day at the zoo without ever seeing the zombie zookeeper again!

As we walked in the exhibit, we saw all kinds of animals.

Owls hooted from their trees, bats flew overhead, and foxes and lemurs roamed around the fake forest floor.

It was actually kind of neat seeing how animals live at night when most of us are sleeping. I was definitely going to write about this for my zoo report!

Desmond, of course, was still searching the place for zombies. He kept thinking he saw the strange zookeeper. Every few minutes I would hear him scream, "Aha! Got you, zombie!"

But it was never him. It was usually just some teacher or class parent. But that didn't stop Desmond.

"Aha!" I heard Desmond scream again for the fourth or fifth time. This time, the teacher he scared ran right out of the exhibit! I couldn't help but laugh.

That was when it happened: A perfectly good time at the zoo took a turn for the weird.

We spotted the zombie zookeeper.

He was walking with a bucket full
of something slimy and gross.
Like *really* gross.

And this is where the story began. I told you I needed to start from the beginning, right? Otherwise, would you have believed that *I*, *Andres Miedoso*, would be trying to trap a zombie zookeeper in the dark?

Probably not.

But Desmond and I were there, watching the zombie zookeeper. When he was close enough, Desmond jumped out of the darkness and screamed, "AHA! We've got you!"

And just like everybody else had, the zombie zookeeper jumped too. And guess where that bucket of slimy grossness ended up?

Yep.

All over me.

CHAPTER NINE

SNIFF

Being covered in goo is not fun. I've been slimed before by a ghost, but that was a different story. Being covered in the goo that nocturnal animals like to eat is possibly one of the least fun things *ever*.

And I couldn't scream.

Screaming would have meant opening my mouth. And there was no way I was going to do that. So, I just stood there, dripping with icky stuff.

That's when I heard the noise behind me.

SNIFF SNIFF sniff

SNIFF

SNIFF

SNIFF

SNIFF

It wasn't like one animal was sniffing. It sounded like fifty animals were sniffing the air all at once. It didn't take me long to realize they were sniffing *me*!

SNIFF SNIFF

sniff

SNIFF SNIFF

"Oh no!" I whimpered through half-clenched teeth.

All of a sudden, every nocturnal animal was swooping in! Bats licked

my hair, foxes tugged at my shoelaces, and a giant owl cried and snatched at my hood. It was trying to lift me off the ground and fly me away!

"Desmond! Help!" I shrieked.

But it wasn't Desmond who came to my rescue. It was the zombie zookeeper! He stepped in and calmly removed each animal. He picked up the fox and said, "No."

He waved the bats away with a weird squeaking sound. Then he cried out just like an owl, and that owl flew away and left me alone.

"Come . . . with . . . me," the zombie said. And normally, I would never listen to a zombie, but something told me that I should listen to this one.

After all, he had saved my life . . . *twice* in one day!

Desmond and I followed him outside, where the other zookeeper Peggy was standing. The zombie handed me a towel and said, "Sorry."

Peggy looked at us and frowned. "Well, kids," she said, "I guess I have some explaining to do."

CHAPTER TEN

ZOOMBIE

It turns out that Peggy already knew about the zombie. He works at the zoo! Everyone calls him "Zoombie."

Desmond and I didn't know this before, but zombies make great zookeepers. They can speak to all the animals. (Don't ask me how.)

They can clean windows underwater because they don't need to breathe. And they don't mind cleaning up the really stinky number twos!

Also, zombies are never grossed out by the slimy, icky food they have to feed the animals.

The best part is that the animals love Zoombie. And so do the other zookeepers, like Peggy. She told us most people are too busy looking at all the cool animals. No one ever noticed that Zoombie was a zombie, other than Desmond Cole.

Anyway, when it comes to zombie zookeepers . . . well, Zoombie is a keeper!

Now whenever Desmond and I go to the zoo, we have a great time. Zoombie always invites the animals to come out, so we never miss seeing any of them.

Plus, he makes sure those peacocks never bother me. Or steal my lunch.

He's so cool that I almost wish I had a special zombie buddy in my life all the time. . . .

Almost!